MATTHEW THE MAGICIAN

Matthew got a cape. He got a hat.

Matthew wanted to be a magician.

Matthew got some magnets. He got a box of pins.

He picked up one pin. He picked up two pins.
He picked up three pins. Was it magic?

No, it was a magnet!

Matthew got a little magnet. He made the little magnet wiggle.
He made the little magnet move. Was it magic?

No, it was a magnet!

Matthew bumped the box of pins.
Matthew made a mess!

He picked up the pins. No more mess!

Was it magic?

No, it was a magnet!

Matthew was missing!

Where did Matthew go?

Something wiggled. Someone giggled. Was it magic?

No, it was Matthew!